Duckat

The author acknowledges with gratitude the assistance
of the Choysa Bursary, which enabled her
to complete this book.

For Sam

Originally published in 1992 in New Zealand by Ashton Scholastic, Ltd.

ISBN 0-590-45456-0
ISBN 0-590-29043-6 (meets NASTA specifications)
Text copyright © 1992 by Gaelyn Gordon.
Illustrations copyright © 1992 by Chris Gaskin.
All rights reserved. Published by Scholastic Inc.,
730 Broadway, New York, NY 10003, by arrangement with
Ashton Scholastic, Ltd.

1 2 3 4 5 6 7 8 9 10   08   00 99 98 97 96 95 94 93

Printed in the U.S.A.

Duckat

By Gaelyn Gordon
Illustrated by Chris Gaskin

SCHOLASTIC INC.
New York   Toronto   London   Auckland   Sydney

On Monday morning,
Mabel opened her door.
There was a duck on the back step.

"Hello," said Mabel.
"Meow," said the duck.
"Odd," said Mabel.
"Very odd."

She put it in the lily pond.
But it hated that. "Yeowwww!" it yelled.

4

"I've never been scratched
by a duck before," said Mabel.

The duck would not eat bread,
but it drank a bowl full of milk.

It caught five mice
and gave them to Mabel.
"Odd," said Mabel.
"Very odd."

When the duck wasn't looking,
Mabel hid the mice in the bread bin.
"I don't want to hurt its feelings," she said.

The duck hid under the sofa
and pounced at Mabel's toes.
"Well!" said Mabel.
"You are a very different sort of duck."

When Mabel started knitting,
the duck joined in.
It growled at the balls of yarn
and stalked them like a mighty hunter.
It rolled them over the floor.
"Odd," said Mabel.
"Very odd."

9

The duck curled up by the fire and purred a bit.
Then it went to sleep.

"That duck," said Mabel, "thinks it's a cat."
She got out her Doctor Book and looked up:
What to do for a duck
that thinks it is a cat.

When the duck woke up,
there were pictures all around it.
There were pictures of ducks
labeled DUCK,
and pictures of cats
labeled CAT.

12

The duck changed the labels over.

"Well!" said Mabel.
"What do I have to do
to show you that you're a duck?"
The duck shrugged.
"Meow," it said.

Mabel took the duck outside.

"Cats climb trees," she said.
The duck climbed the tree.
"Odd," said Mabel.
"Very odd."

"Cats wash behind their ears," said Mabel.
The duck washed behind its ears.
"Odd," said Mabel.
"Very odd."

15

Butch, the dog who lived next door,
bounced through the gate.
"Dogs chase cats," said Mabel.

"But they chase ducks, too."

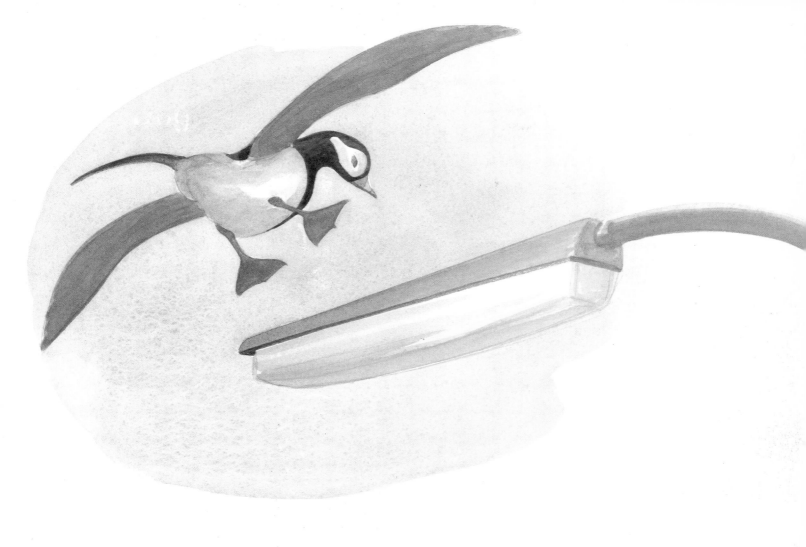

Butch nearly got the duck,
but it flew up to the top of the lamppost.
"You couldn't do that if you were a cat,"
said Mabel.

17

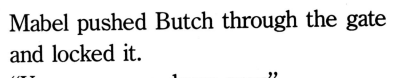

Mabel pushed Butch through the gate
and locked it.
"You can come down now,"
Mabel told the duck.
"Meow," said the duck.

18

"Cats can't fly down
from lampposts," said Mabel,
"and I don't have a ladder.
If you are a cat,
you'll just have to stay up there."

The duck flew down.

It looked up at Mabel.
"Quack," it said.

"You were only joking, weren't you?" said Mabel.
"Quack," said the duck,
and it went for a swim in the lily pond to cool off.

On Tuesday morning,
Mabel opened her door.
There was a cat on the back step.
"Hello," said Mabel.
"Quack!" said the cat.

"Odd," said the duck.
"Very odd."